A FROG INSIDE MY HAT

COMPILED BY

FAY ROBINSON

PICTURES BY

CYD MOORE

Troll Medallion

Title from "Notice." From *One at a Time* by David McCord. Copyright 1952 by David McCord. By permission of Little, Brown and Company.

A FIRST BOOK OF POEMS

For Emily and Daniel *F.R.*

For Branden, who has harbored
his share of squirmy creatures
under his baseball cap. *C.M.*

Copyright © 1993 Fay Robinson

Illustration copyright © 1993 Cyd Moore

**Published by Troll Medallion, an imprint of
Troll Associates.**

All rights reserved. No part of this book may be
used or reproduced in any manner whatsoever
without written permission from the publisher.
Designed by Leslie Bauman.

Printed in Mexico.

10   9   8   7   6   5   4   3   2

Library of Congress Cataloging-in-Publication Data

A Frog inside my hat / edited by Fay Robinson;
pictures by Cyd Moore.
      p. cm.
   Summary: A collection of short whimsical
poems by such authors as Lucille Clifton, John
Ciardi, Russell Hoban, and Sylvia Plath.
   ISBN 0-8167-3129-2 (lib. bdg.)
   ISBN 0-8167-3130-6 (pbk.)
   1. Children's poetry.   [1. Poetry—Collections.]
I. Robinson, Fay.   II. Moore, Cyd, ill.
PN6109.97F76   1993   808.81′0083—dc20
  93-22200

CONTENTS

Notice

I have a dog,
I had a cat.
I've got a frog
Inside my hat.

David McCord

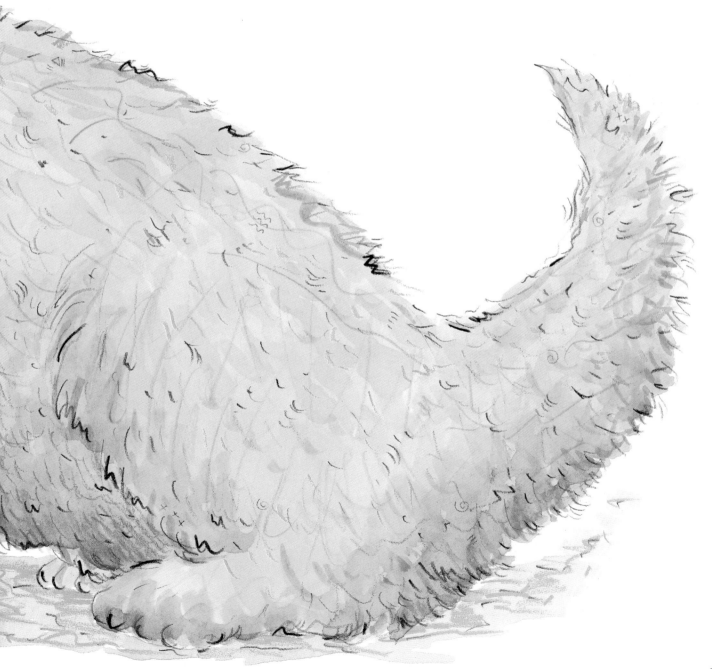

April

Rain is good
for washing leaves
and stones and bricks and
even eyes,
and if you hold
your head just so
you can almost see
the tops of skies.

Lucille Clifton

10

Nest Eggs

Here in the fork
    The brown nest is seated;
Four little blue eggs
    The mother keeps heated.

Robert Louis Stevenson

Baby Chick

Peck
   peck
      peck

on the warm brown egg.
OUT comes a neck.
OUT comes a leg.

How
   does
      a chick,
who's not been about,
discover the trick
of how to get out?

Aileen Fisher

There Was an Old Man With a Beard

There was an Old Man with a beard,
Who said, "It is just as I feared!—
   Two Owls and a Hen,
   Four Larks and a Wren,
Have all built their nests in my beard!"

Edward Lear

The Dragonfly

A dragonfly sat
 on my nose
I wish it had sat
 on my toes
I guess nobody
 ever knows
Where a dragonfly will sit

Nikki Giovanni

Bird Talk

"Think…" said the robin,
"Think…" said the jay,
sitting in the garden,
talking one day.

"Think about people—
the way they grow:
they don't have feathers
at all, you know.

They don't eat beetles
they don't grow wings
they don't like sitting
on wires and things."

"Think!" said the robin.
"Think!" said the jay.
"Aren't people funny
to be that way?"

Aileen Fisher

19

Frog

The frog,
when he's alone
and sad,
writes poems
on
his lily pad:

Froggies are green
bluefish are blue,
guppies are sweet,
and so are you.

N. M. Bodecker

The Lizard

The Lizard is a timid thing
That cannot dance or fly or sing;
He hunts for bugs beneath the floor
And longs to be a dinosaur.

John Gardner

Snail

Little snail,
Dreaming you go.
Weather and rose
Is all you know.

Langston Hughes

Ants Live Here

Ants live here
by the curb stone,
        see?
They worry a lot
about giants like
        me.

Lilian Moore

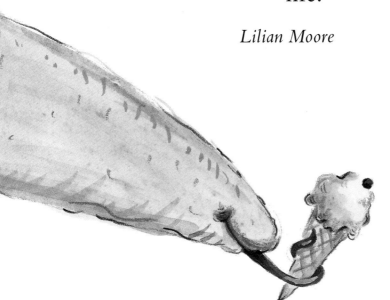

Be Kind to Dumb Animals

There once was an ape in a zoo
Who looked out through the bars and saw—YOU!
    Do you think it's fair
     To give poor apes a scare?
I think it's a mean thing to do!

John Ciardi

There's a Black Sheep in the Shower

There's a black sheep in the shower
Having a shampoo.
The water is so very cold
That he has turned bright blue.

Alice Gilbert

The Purple Cow

I never saw a Purple Cow,
    I never hope to see one;
But I can tell you, anyhow,
    I'd rather see than be one.

Gelett Burgess

The Birthday Cow

Happy Mooday to you,
Happy Mooday to you.
Happy Mooday,
Dear Yooday.
Happy Mooday to you.

Eve Merriam

29

Oodles of Noodles

I love noodles. Give me oodles.
Make a mound up to the sun.
Noodles are my favorite foodles.
I eat noodles by the ton.

Lucia and James L. Hymes, Jr.

30

Mickey Jones

When Mickey Jones
Eats ice cream cones
He gets himself so sticky,

It's never known
Which one is cone
And which is only Mickey.

X.J. Kennedy

Egg-Thoughts

Soft-boiled

I do not like the way you slide,
I do not like your soft inside,
I do not like you many ways,
And I could do for many days
Without a soft-boiled egg.

Sunny-Side-Up

With their yolks and whites all runny
They are looking at me funny.

Russell Hoban

I Eat My Peas With Honey

I eat my peas with honey;
I've done it all my life.
It makes the peas taste funny,
But it keeps them on the knife.

Author Unknown

Although He Didn't Like the Taste

Although he didn't like the taste,
George brushed his teeth with pickle paste.
Not ever was his mouth so clean,
Not ever were his teeth so green.

Arnold Lobel

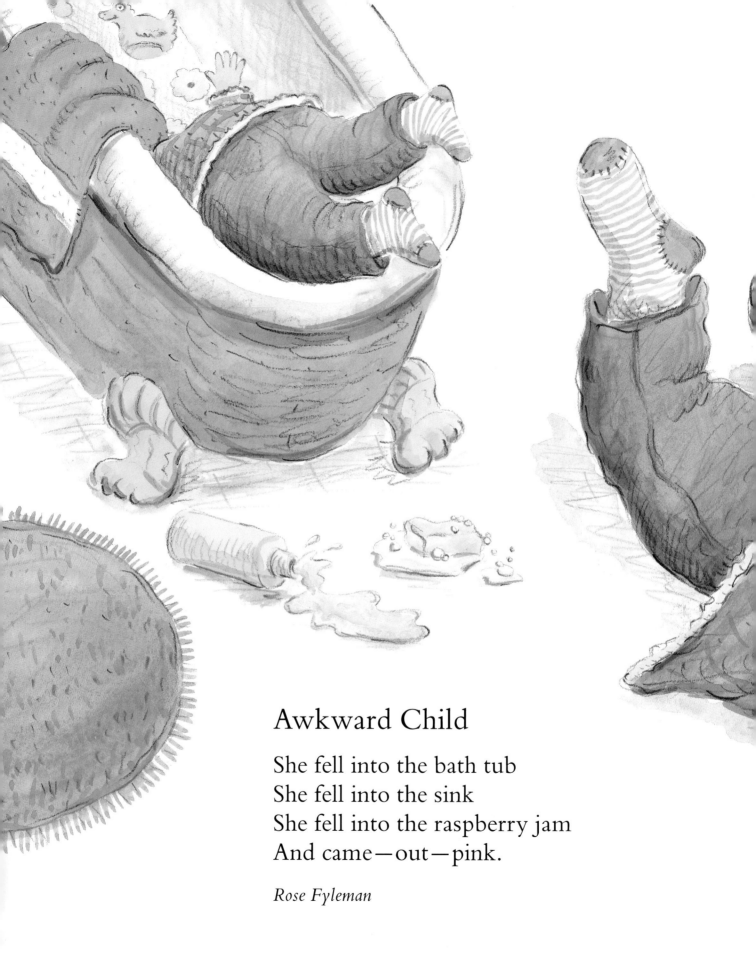

Awkward Child

She fell into the bath tub
She fell into the sink
She fell into the raspberry jam
And came—out—pink.

Rose Fyleman

My Sister Laura

My sister Laura's bigger than me
And lifts me up quite easily.
I can't lift her, I've tried and tried;
She must have something heavy inside.

Spike Milligan

Some People I Know

Some people I know
fill up the whole chair.
They don't share.

Richard J. Margolis

My Legs and I

I say to my legs,
    "Legs," I say,
"Let's go out
    To run and play."

So off we go,
    My legs and I,
Skipping, romping,
    Jumping high.

Then I say to my legs,
    "Legs," I say,
"I'm much too tired
    To run and play."

So legs and I
    Toward home we go,
Walking, walking,
    Slow, slow, slow.

Leland B. Jacobs

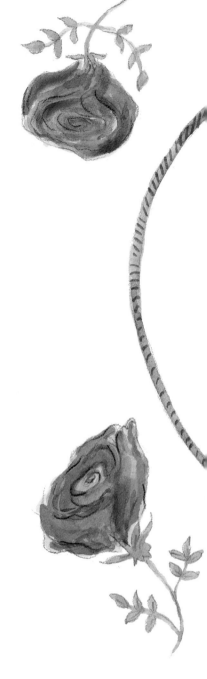

I Am Rose

I am Rose my eyes are blue
I am Rose and who are you?
I am Rose and when I sing
I am Rose like anything.

Gertrude Stein

Sometimes

Sometimes
when I skip or hop
or when I'm
    jumping

Suddenly
I like to stop
and listen to me
    thumping.

Lilian Moore

Night Scare

There aren't any ghosts.
There aren't any.
There aren't any gho—
Well…not too many.

Judith Viorst

44

Why Rabbits Jump

"Why are you rabbits jumping so?
 Now please tell why, tell why."
"We jump to see the big round moon
 Up in the sky, the sky."

An old Japanese rhyme

I Do Not Mind You, Winter Wind

I do not mind you, Winter Wind
when you come whirling by,
to tickle me with snowflakes
drifting softly from the sky.

I do not even mind you
when you nibble at my skin,
scrambling over all of me
attempting to get in.

But when you bowl me over
and I land on my behind,
then I must tell you, Winter Wind,
I mind…I really mind!

Jack Prelutsky

Winter Clothes

Under my hood I have a hat
And under that
My hair is flat.
Under my coat
My sweater's blue.
My sweater's red.
I'm wearing two.
My muffler muffles to my chin
And round my neck
And then tucks in.
My gloves were knitted
By my aunts.

I've mittens too
And pants
And pants
And boots
And shoes
With socks inside.
The boots are rubber, red and wide.
And when I walk
I must not fall
Because I can't get up at all.

Karla Kuskin

Furry Bear

If I were a bear,
  And a big bear too,
I shouldn't much care
  If it froze or snew;
I shouldn't much mind
  If it snowed or friz—
I'd be all fur-lined
  With a coat like his!

A. A. Milne

Lying on Things

After it snows
I go and lie on things.

I lie on my back
And make snow-angel wings.

I lie on my front
And powder-puff my nose.

I *always* lie on things
Right after it snows.

Dennis Lee

Bears

Bears
have few cares.
When the wind blows cold
   and the snow drifts deep
they sleep and sleep and sleep and sleep.

Elizabeth Coatsworth

In an Elephant Bed

In an Elephant Bed
you go where you please.
You pick bananas
right out of the trees.

An Elephant Bed
is where kings ride.
It's cool as a pool
in the shade inside.
You can climb up the trunk
and slide down behind.
Everyone knows
elephants don't mind!

Sylvia Plath

57

Who's Afraid?

I went to sleep last night
　　And dreamed.

They tell me that I woke
　　And screamed.

I was not really scared.
　　Not me!

I simply called so they
　　Could see

The witch who leaped up from
　　The floor

And flew right through my
　　Bedroom door.

If she should come again
　　Tonight,

I'll scream again with all
　　My might.

But just so they can come
　　And see.

And not because I'm scared—
　　Not me!

Lucia and James L. Hymes, Jr.

59

Bedtime Stories

"Tell me a story,"
Says Witch's Child.

"About the Beast
So fierce and wild.

About a Ghost
That shrieks and groans.

A Skeleton
That rattles bones.

About a Monster
Crawly–creepy.

Something nice
To make me sleepy."

Lilian Moore

Morning

Everyone is tight asleep,
I think I'll sing a tune,
And if I sing it loud enough
I'll wake up someone—soon!

Myra Cohn Livingston

ACKNOWLEDGMENTS

Grateful acknowledgment is made to the following for permission to reprint the poems in this book. Every effort has been made to secure the necessary permissions and make full acknowledgment for their use. If notified of any errors, the publisher will gladly make the necessary corrections in future editions.

Addison-Wesley Publishing Company, Inc. for "Oodles of Noodles" and "Who's Afraid?" from *Oodles of Noodles* by Lucia and James Hymes, Jr., © 1964 by Addison-Wesley Publishing Company, Inc.; and "I Am Rose" (excerpt) from *The World is Round* by Gertrude Stein, © 1966 by Addison-Wesley Publishing Company, Inc. Reprinted with permission of the publisher.

Atheneum Publishers for "Night Scare" by Judith Viorst. Reprinted with permission of Atheneum Publishers, an imprint of Macmillan Publishing Company, from *If I Were in Charge of the World and Other Worries* by Judith Viorst. Copyright © 1981 by Judith Viorst.

Alice Gilbert AvRutick for "There's a Black Sheep in the Shower" (excerpt from "Household Pets") from *Poems from Sharon's Lunchbox* by Alice Gilbert, published by Delacorte Press, copyright 1972 by Alice Gilbert. Reprinted by permission of the author.

Kate Barnes for "Bears" by Elizabeth Coatsworth. Reprinted by permission of Kate Barnes.

Georges Borchardt, Inc. for "The Lizard" from *A Child's Bestiary* by John Gardner. Reprinted by permission of Georges Borchardt, Inc. Copyright © 1977 by Boskydell Artists Ltd.

Dover Publications for "The Purple Cow" from *The Purple Cow and Other Nonsense* by Gelett Burgess. Reprinted by permission of Dover Publications.

Dutton Children's Books for "Furry Bear" from *Now We Are Six* by A.A. Milne. Copyright 1927 by E.P. Dutton, renewed © 1955 by A.A. Milne. Used by permission of Dutton Children's Books, a division of Penguin Books USA Inc.

Faber and Faber Ltd. for "In an Elephant Bed," excerpt from *The Bed Book* by Sylvia Plath. Reprinted by permission of Faber and Faber Ltd. (For Canadian rights.)

Aileen Fisher for "Baby Chick" from *Runny Days, Sunny Days* by Aileen Fisher, and "Bird Talk" from *Up the Windy Hill* by Aileen Fisher, copyrights renewed. Reprinted by permission of the author.

Greenwillow Books for "Although he didn't like the taste..." from *Whiskers and Rhymes* by Arnold Lobel, copyright © 1985 by Arnold Lobel; and "I Do Not Mind You, Winter Wind" from *It's Snowing! It's Snowing!* by Jack Prelutsky, copyright © 1984 by Jack Prelutsky. By permission of Greenwillow Books, a division of William Morrow & Company, Inc.

HarperCollins Publishers for "Egg Thoughts" (excerpt) from *Egg Thoughts and other Frances Songs* by Russell Hoban, copyright © 1964, 1972 by Russell Hoban; "Winter Clothes" from *The Rose on My Cake* by Karla Kuskin, copyright © 1964 by Karla Kuskin; "Some People I Know" from *Only the Moon and Me* by Richard J. Margolis, copyright © 1969 by Richard J. Margolis; and "In an Elephant Bed," excerpt 12 lines from *The Bed Book* by Sylvia Plath, copyright © 1976 by Ted Hughes. Selections reprinted by permission of HarperCollins Publishers.

Henry Holt and Company for "April" from *Everett Anderson's Year* by Lucille Clifton, copyright © 1974 by Lucille Clifton; and "My Legs and I" from *Is Somewhere Always Far Away* by Leland B. Jacobs, copyright © 1967 by Leland B. Jacobs. Poems reprinted by permission of Henry Holt and Company, Inc.